SLÁINE
The King

**Pat Mills, Mike McMahon &
Glenn Fabry**
**With Angie Mills &
Anthony Williams**

TITAN BOOKS
in association with *2000 AD*

SLÁINE THE KING

ISBN 1 84023 416 4

Published by Titan Books, a division of Titan Publishing Group Ltd.
144 Southwark St
London SE1 0UP
In association with Rebellion

A CIP catalogue record for this title is available from the British Library.

First edition: February 2002
1 3 5 7 9 10 8 6 4 2

Cover illustration by Glenn Fabry.

Printed in Italy.

Other *2000 AD* titles now available from Titan Books:

Judge Dredd: Emerald Isle (ISBN: 1 84023 341 9)
Judge Dredd: Death Aid (ISBN: 1 84023 344 3)
Judge Dredd: Goodnight Kiss (ISBN: 1 84023 346 X)
Judge Dredd Featuring Judge Death (ISBN: 1 84023 386 9)
Judge Dredd: Helter Skelter (ISBN: 1 84023 348 6)

The Complete Ballad of Halo Jones (ISBN: 1 84023 342 7)
The Complete D.R. & Quinch (ISBN: 1 84023 345 1)
A.B.C. Warriors: The Mek-Nificent Seven (ISBN: 1 84023 347 8)

To order telephone 01536 764 646 ext. 21

What did you think of this book? We love to hear from our readers. Please email us at: readerfeedback@titanemail.com, or write to us at the above address.

Artwork by Angie Mills

One of *2000 AD*'s most popular and enduring characters, the Celtic warrior Sláine's story began on the 20th August, 1983, in Prog #330 ('*The Time Monster*'). Billed as a "new sword and sorcery saga", and featuring an Angie Mills cover and artwork, prolific *2000 AD* author Pat Mills had created a hero who would return to the pages of the Galaxy's Greatest Comic time and time again, as readers were immediately hooked by *Sláine*'s fusion of violent action-fantasy and elements of Celtic mythology.

Sláine is something of a composite character – the variety of artists who worked on the strip between and including the stories collected here all brought their own vision to the hero: Mike McMahon's tribal realism; David Pugh's Celtic savagery; Mike Collins and Massimo Bellardinelli's romance (the latter also contributed the first graphic version of the Warp Spasm).

Prior to Glenn Fabry (widely considered to be the definitive *Sláine* artist), Angie Mills' brief work on the character was perhaps most influential. A childrens' book illustrator, her primary contribution was to the *sense* of what Sláine ought to be: the original artistic concept of the hero was a rather stereotypical, scowling, behelmeted, muscle-bound barbarian in a traditional fantasy world. Angie Mills questioned these preconceptions, believing them hackneyed and outdated, and instead created a handsome human character, drawn in a primarily illustrative, rather than action-based, style.

This style was revised, improved and ultimately immortalised by Glenn Fabry. A freelance illustrator prior to his work on *Sláine*, Fabry captured and embellished all of the elements which had shaped the look of the character, and presented us with a supremely tough and violent, yet roguish and all-too-human hero.

Meanwhile, author Pat Mills' flair for mixing violent action with strands of Celtic mythology, while never losing focus on the character's humanity, guaranteed that the Mills-Fabry team's take on *Sláine* built a fan-base which has ensured our hero's survival to this day.

When I created *2000 AD*, I constantly used European, rather than British or American comics as my visual role models. It's hardly surprising, therefore, that when I came to creating *Sláine* I would do the same. This time my visual bible was the black and white French fantasy series 'Conquering Armies' from *Metal Hurlant* (the French *Heavy Metal*). The series makes colour seem irrelevant because it turns black and white itself into a beautiful colour of its own, just as Brian Bolland and Frank Miller have done. 'Conquering Armies' is everything I personally adore about comics; it's one of the very few graphic novels I would personally buy. With its tight drawing, fantasy architecture and European sensibility, it is the antithesis of current Anglo-American comic trends.

I gave my then wife, artist Angela Kincaid, 'Conquering Armies' as the style I required for *Sláine*. With no comics knowledge or preconceptions, and with a background in fantasy book illustration, she followed it to the letter, adding some humour and a hero that was very much her personal creation. For the first time in *2000 AD's* history, a hero looked handsome by female criteria rather than male and actually dared to smile. She created an opening episode which exceeded *Judge Dredd* in the popularity polls; the first and only *2000 AD* story to achieve this.

Subsequent *Sláine* artists did excellent work – notably Mike McMahon on 'Sky Chariots'. Angela's reaction was highly enthusiastic. Mike is often called an artist's artist, and an artistic eye sees what goes into the conception, whereas the rest of us just sit back and consume. I wasn't sure how 'Sky Chariots' would go down with the readers, but I was guided by Angela's judgement. Many readers were totally crazy about it; regarding it as Mike's best work ever; others reacted in the completely opposite way, which infuriated me. Seen now, in its entirety, I think they might change their minds and recognise 'Sky Chariots' for the ground-breaking piece of work it is.

Even so, I finally had to admit that the story was moving away from the visual foundations Angela had laid down. Even though it was still popular, I decided – despite editorial protests – to stop the strip until I found a new artist who could restore Angela's vision. The editor offered me the choice of two very talented and extremely successful British artists currently working for America, but I had to

Artwork by Glenn Fabry

say no. Their American orientation was the complete opposite of 'Conquering Armies' and because they were so well established they would be unlikely to adapt to what they would rightly see, from their point of view, as a stiff or heavy illustrative style. And so my long search continued, until artist Bryan Talbot mentioned he knew a highly talented young comic artist called Glenn Fabry, who was currently working in a gas station.

"What's his style?" I asked guardedly.
"I'd describe him as the British Moebius," Bryan replied. There was a sharp intake of breath from me.

Glenn's work soon confirmed he has a great deal in common with France's greatest strip artist. I was knocked out by Glenn's talent and still am. Overruling sabotage attempts from the editorial regime at that time who, incredibly, said they thought Glenn's anatomy was "poor", I went ahead and wrote *Sláine* stories for him which culminated in 'Sláine the King'. Glenn went far beyond Angela's episode one and 'Conquering Armies' and took the series to new heights. His Sláine has heroism, handsome looks and a style that gives him iconic status. His fantasy architecture is so imaginative, it seems almost "channeled"; notably in an earlier story, 'The Tomb of Grimnismal'. His sensitive facial expressions are pure genius, creating that rare thing in comics: pictures that talk to you. And, of course, his anatomy is sublime!

'Sláine the King' sets the standard for *Sláine*'s even greater success in colour with new sagas by artists such as Simon Bisley, Dermot Power and Glenn himself. These highly popular *Sláine* albums have now been published throughout Europe and led the way for other *2000 AD* characters to follow. For all of this, I am aware of the huge debt both I and the character owe to Glenn. Not least because I know *Sláine* took so much out of him personally – as it tends to do with many of the *Sláine* artists. This may be because *Sláine* is not a typical comic book and therefore its rules are different in so many ways. For instance, I will risk showing Sláine in a negative or even absurd way if it is faithful to the chaotic Celtic truth. My sources are too demanding, too esoteric, too personal, and I am too driven by the muse for me to do otherwise. Out of a deep respect for these wondrous sources, I have tried, not always as hard as I should have done, to resist attempts by uncomprehending editors, artists and even some readers to transform the saga into the British equivalent of *Conan*. I believe in 'Sláine the King', at least, Glenn and I succeeded.

Pat Mills, November 2001

GLOSSARY

CARNUN	*The Horned God*, Lord of the Beasts.
CROM-CRUACH	*The Worm God*, Lord of the Mounds.
DANU	*The Earth Goddess.*
DRUIDS	Priests of the Northern tribes.
DRUNE LORDS	Evil Priest-Kings of the Southern tribes.
EARTH POWER	The spiral force that runs through the *Weird Stones* (Megaliths). Also known as the *Earth Serpent.*
HALF-DEAD	Warriors killed but trapped between the worlds.
HERO-HARNESS	Worn by warped warriors, so their clothes don't rip during a spasm.
LUG	*The Sun God.* The Sun and Earth are worshipped by the Northern tribes.
OGHAMS	Early form of writing. Also a sign language.
RED BRANCH	Sláine's tribe's greatest warriors.
SALMON LEAP	Jumping your own height. A Sessair battle-skill — like shield-jumping and spear-catching.
SESSAIR	Sláine's tribe.
SKULL-SWORDS	Drune soldiers.
SLOUGH	Drune leader who has sloughed (shed) his skin.
SOURLAND	Land warped by sorcery.
THE LORD WEIRD SLOUGH FEG	*Supreme Drune*, thousands of years old.
TIR-NAN-OG	*The Land of the Young.*
TRIBES OF THE EARTH GODDESS	The legendary Northern tribes, including the Sessair.
WARP SPASM	A strange and terrifying battle-frenzy, much worse than a Beserker fury. Caused by *Earth Power* which some warriors can warp through their bodies.

Sláine

— WARRIOR'S DAWN.
IT WAS NEARLY SAMAIN AS SLÁINE OF
THE SESSAIR AND I, UKKO, HIS DWARF,
RODE ON THROUGH THE SOURLAND —
THE SWAMP WHERE THE DRUNES
WARPED ALL THE POWER FROM THE
EARTH — AND THE 'HALF-DEAD', TRAPPED
BETWEEN THE WORLDS, LIE IN WAIT
FOR THE UNWARY...

WHY DON'T
YOU GO
BACK TO THE
BOG YOU
CRAWLED
OUT OF?

THAT'S VERY
NICE! LEAVE ME
IN THE MIDDLE OF
THE SOURLAND!
IT'S NOT MY
FAULT YOU GOT
KICKED OUT OF
YOUR TRIBE!

SCRIPT:
PAT MILLS
ART:
MIKE McMAHON
LETTERING:
TOM FRAME

WE STOPPED
TO REST OUR
MOUNTS.

I THOUGHT
HAVING A
FOOL FOR A
COMPANION
WOULD BRING
ME LUCK.

EVERYTHING
I'VE DONE FOR
YOU – AND THAT'S
ALL THE GRATITUDE
I GET!

WOULD
YOU LIKE
TO BUY A
SADDLE,
SIR?

WHAT
DID I
SAY?

SLÁINE ALWAYS
RIDES BAREBACK.
IN HIS TRIBE
IT'S CONSIDERED
THE HEIGHT OF
EFFEMINACY
AND SHAME TO
WEAR A
SADDLE

I BEG
YOUR
PARDON,
LORD. I
MEANT NO
SLUR ON YOUR
CHARACTER.

HE MUST
HAVE A
HIDE OF
BRONZE!

HIS TRIBE
MUST BE
GREAT
WARRIORS.

AND HE
BELONGS TO
THE RED BRANCH –
GREATEST OF THEM
ALL. HE'S TOLD ME
SUCH STORIES...
WHICH YOU CAN
HEAR IF YOU
GIVE ME A
HORN OF ALE.

THOUGH HE WAS NOT ALONE... FOR HE WAS SURROUNDED BY HIGH HEROES OF THE PAST...

THOSE HEROES ARE CERTAINLY 'HIGH'!

AT LAST... CATHBAD REMOVED A CRYSTAL SLAB FROM THE ROOF...

SLÁINE IS VERY YOUNG TO BE WARPED. I HOPE HE CAN SURVIVE THIS...

AT EXACTLY MIDWINTER, A SHAFT OF SUNLIGHT SHOT DOWN THE PASSAGE INTO THE CENTRAL CHAMBER... ITS RAYS WIDENING OUT LIKE A *RED BRANCH*.

AND THE POWER OF THE SUN AND EARTH WARPED THROUGH HIM!

MOMENTS LATER...

LUG BE PRAISED!

NOW SLÁINE WAS ENTITLED TO ENTER THE GREAT ROUND HALL AND WEAR A HERO-HARNESS – THAT WOULD EXPAND WITH HIS WARP-SPASM.

AND CATHBAD MADE PROPHECIES ABOUT SLÁINE.

I SEE A HERO SWINGING A CRIMSON AXE, RED-MOUTHED SCREAMS, MOUNDS OF FALLEN, SMASHED SHIELDS, RAVENS GNAWING ENEMIES' NECKS ON THE FIELD OF SLAUGHTER.

SOUNDS LIKE A PROMISING FUTURE, LAD.

AND I CAN ALSO SEE A RAT-LIKE DWARF...! STRANGE...! BUT I'VE BEEN HAVING TROUBLE WITH MY VISIONS LATELY.

SO WHAT HAPPENED THEN?

I WAS THROWN OUT OF MY TRIBE AND BECAME A WANDERING VAGABOND... A PROUD WARRIOR SUNK LOW...

NEVER MIND, SLÁINE. THERE'S ONE RAY OF SUNSHINE LEFT... YOU'VE STILL GOT ME!

NEXT PROG: SKY CHARIOTS

"**And it came to pass that . . .** Slàine and I encountered a wealthy man who wanted us to rescue his daughter Medb, a Priestess of the Badb, who was due to be sacrificed at Samain. This we duly did, only to discover that she did not want to be rescued. Indeed, so infuriated was she by the rescue that, she sought aid from her former captor, to hurry the demise of Slàine and myself. And so, unbeknownst to us, her former captor Slough Trot, the most powerful Drune Lord of Slough Feg, was sent out along with a company of Skull Swords, to hunt us down . . ."

OUR BEAST.

THESE PEOPLE ARE STARVING TO DEATH.

VERY SAD. BUT WHAT'S IT GOT TO DO WITH US?

SHUT UP, DWARF.

HERE, FELLOW... TAKE THE HAIRY ONE TO YOUR KILLING POUND.

SO MUCH MEAT! WE'RE SAVED!

THAT NIGHT THE VILLAGERS CELEBRATED WITH A FEAST.

YOU SHOULDN'T SAVE THE LIVES OF PEOPLE FATED TO DIE, SLÁINE! THAT'S CHEATING THE GODS!

YOU'RE WELCOME TO STAY HERE, SLÁINE.

SORRY, MADOG, THE DWARF AND I ARE DRIFTERS, CARING ONLY THAT WE'VE ENOUGH TO EAT AND DRINK...ESPECIALLY DRINK...

OF COURSE! CAW! MORE MEAD FOR OUR GUESTS!

BUT AS CAW STEPPED OUTSIDE...

COME HERE, BOY!

SKULL-SWORDS!

CONTINUED NEXT PROG.

AS CAW APPROACHED HE COULD SMELL THE DRUNE'S OVERPOWERING STENCH — KNOWN AS THE 'MYSTIC AURA'...

HE REMEMBERED THE NIGHTMARE TALES HE'D BEEN TOLD OF WHAT WAS UNDERNEATH THOSE FUR ROBES...

...AND HERE WAS A DRUNE THAT HAD REACHED THE SUPREME RANK OF 'SLOUGH' — SHEDDING HIS SKIN...

THE DRUNES HAD MASTERED *EARTH POWER* — USING IT FOR EVIL — BUT THEY HAD PAID A TERRIBLE PRICE IN FESTERING DECAY...

THE SKULL-SWORDS LOOKED ON — THEIR *BREATH MASKS* PROTECTING THEM FROM THEIR MASTER'S FUMES.

SPEAK UP, BOY!

CAW SHEAF-HAIR, SON OF MADOG STAG-SHANKS! LORD...IT IS ONLY A HAIRY ONE WE ARE EATING IN THE HALL.

AND HOW CAME YOU BY THIS BEAST?

A MAN CAME TO OUR VILLAGE AND JUST...GAVE IT TO US!

BAH! YOU EXPECT ME TO BELIEVE SUCH AN UNLIKELY STORY?

KILL HIM!

NO!

MOMENTS LATER...

SURROUND THE HALL. LET NO-ONE ESCAPE!

MEANWHILE, INSIDE...

THE DRUNES ARE DESTROYING THE LAND. THERE IS TALK OF A GREAT FLOOD — A RAGNORAK — THAT WILL MEAN *THE END OF OUR WORLD.* THEY HAVE TO BE STOPPED!

ONLY MEN LIKE YOU — FROM THE TRIBES OF THE EARTH GODDESS — HAVE THE COURAGE TO FACE THE DRUNES. IF YOU WERE TO STAY... IF... *SLÁINE!* YOU'RE NOT LISTENING TO ME!

MADOG, MY FRIEND. I HATE THE DRUNES AS MUCH AS YOU, BUT I TAKE EACH DAY AS IT COMES. POLITICS BORE ME. I'M HEADING NORTH.

BUT I DON'T WANT TO!

YOU DON'T HAVE TO COME WITH ME.

A DWARF NEEDS A PROTECTOR IN THESE TROUBLED TIMES.

LET'S TALK OF MORE IMPORTANT MATTERS, MADOG. LIKE WHY MY DRINKING HORN IS EMPTY. WHAT'S HAPPENED TO THAT SON OF YOURS?

YES... CAW'S BEEN A LONG WHILE.

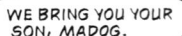

WE BRING YOU YOUR SON, MADOG.

WE SUSPECTED YOU'D BEEN EATING THE FORBIDDEN FLESH.

IT SEEMS WE WERE WRONG.

MADOG STAG-SHANKS WAS A MILD MAN — BUT WHEN HE SAW HIS DEAD SON, SOMETHING INSIDE HIM SNAPPED.

MURDERERS!

EVERYTHING HAPPENED VERY QUICKLY. MADOG'S WIFE SCREAMED —

HIS KIN LEAPT TO THEIR FEET —

AND WERE CUT DOWN BY THE SKULL-SWORDS.

AT THE SAME TIME, SLÁINE WAS MOVING, LIFTING THE TABLE, SCATTERING FOOD AND DRINK —

DOWN! GET D·O·W·N!

USING IT AS A GIGANTIC SHIELD —

CRUSHING THE SKULL-SWORDS INTO THE WALL, BREAKING RIBS AND SNAPPING NECKS.

UKKO! BRAIN-BITER — TO ME!

I'LL PUT YOU IN A WAY YOU'LL MURDER NO MORE!

HE STILL BURNS, LORD.

BRING TUBS OF COLD WATER. WE MUST COOL HIS FIRE OR WHEN HE AWAKES HE'LL HURL HIMSELF ON YOUR SWORDS.

THE WARP-SPASM PASSED...

I'M STILL ALIVE. THERE MUST BE A REASON...

YES. I AM TRAVELLING NORTH BY SKY CHARIOT. I NEED A PERSONAL *BATTLE-SMITER*.

NO THANKS. I COULDN'T STAND THE STENCH.

YOU'LL GROW USED TO MY 'MYSTIC AURA' IN TIME. IT'S A SIGN I'VE REACHED THE SUPREME RANK OF 'SLOUGH'...

...THOUGH YOU CAN WEAR A BREATH-MASK TO PROTECT YOU FROM MY FUMES.

YOU'LL BE PAID WELL FOR THE TASK. AND THE VILLAGERS GIVEN ENOUGH FOOD TO LAST THEM THROUGH THE WINTER.

IF I REFUSE?

GAVRA WILL BE BURNT TO THE GROUND AND YOU AND YOUR DWARF SUFFER THE DEATH OF THE BLOOD EAGLE.

SHORTLY AFTER, WE LEFT WITH SLOUGH THROT.

AT LEAST WE GET A FREE RIDE HOME.

BUT I'VE NEVER FLOWN BEFORE. I DON'T THINK I'D LIKE IT!

IF I HADN'T AGREED, OUR RIBS WOULD HAVE PARTED COMPANY WITH OUR BACKBONES BY NOW.

WE APPROACHED THE NEARBY DOLMEN - ONE OF A NETWORK OF STONES ACROSS TIR-NAN-OG. FROM HERE, SKY CHARIOTS SAILED FOR THE NORTH.

THE DOLMEN ACTED AS A HUGE BATTERY, DRAINING EARTH POWER FROM THE SURROUNDING COUNTRYSIDE...PROVIDING ENERGY FOR THE VESSELS TO RISE AND FALL.

'THOUGH THE POWER WAS NOT EASY TO CONTROL...

OCH!

OUR VESSEL WAS A LARGE MERCHANTMAN – A *CLOUD CURRAGH* – WITH NO LESS THAN THREE DRUNES CONTROLLING ITS *WEIRD STONE*...

WELCOME ABOARD, SLOUGH THROT. *RISE PRAYERS* WILL BE IN ONE HAND'S TIME.

WE GATHERED ON DECK AND KNELT DOWN. THEN THE DRUNE LORD MADE OGHAM SIGNS OVER THE STONE...

IT WOULD RECEIVE POWER FROM THE STANDING STONES AND TRANSMIT IT DURING THE VOYAGE.

O LUG, GREAT GOD OF THE SKY, LOOK AFTER LITTLE UKKO. EVEN IF THE OTHERS GET IT...

...MAKE SURE I'M ALL RIGHT!

SPIRAL ENERGY – KNOWN AS 'THE SERPENT' – POURED FROM THE DOLMEN. FOR A MOMENT NOTHING HAPPENED...

THEN, LO! THE CLOUD CURRAGH LIFTED...

...AND SOARED INTO THE SKY!

THE VESSEL SET COURSE FOR THE NORTH –

I DON'T LIKE IT, SLÁINE. THE DRUNES HAVE VAST POWERS – WHY SHOULD SLOUGH THROT NEED A BATTLE-SMITER? WHO IS HE AFRAID OF...?

...AND WHEN A DRUNE IS AFRAID... THEN IT'S TIME TO FEAR!

NEXT PROG: STRANGE CARGO!

Sláine

SKY CHARIOTS — 4.

FACED WITH THE CHOICE OF THE EXTERMINATION OF HIS FRIENDS IN GAVRA OR BECOMING BATTLE-SMITER (BODYGUARD) TO SLOUGH THROT, SLÁINE RELUCTANTLY AGREED TO PROTECT THE SINISTER DRUNE LORD. NOW, WE TRAVELLED NORTH BY CLOUD CURRAGH...

WE'RE SAILING NORTH-EAST — OVER LYONESSE. I WONDER WHERE SLOUGH THROT'S GOING?

LONG AS WE GET THERE SOON!

LOOK OUT BELOW!

UHHHHH!

SCRIPT:
PAT MILLS
ART:
MIKE McMAHON
LETTERING:
TOM FRAME

SLOUGH THROT WAS HUNGRY.

STUPID BOY! THIS MEAT IS *FRESH!* I ONLY EAT *RANCID* FLESH.

BRING ME SOMETHING OLD AND DECAYING.

AT ONCE, LORD!

HA! HA! YOU'RE SLOUGH THROT'S BODYGUARD, SO YOU'LL HAVE TO TEST HIS FOOD AND MAKE SURE IT'S ROTTEN ENOUGH!

SILENCE, DWARF!

THAT WON'T BE NECESSARY, SLÁINE. THIS REPLACEMENT MEAT HAS REACHED A FINE STATE OF DECOMPOSITION!

BUT YOU NEGLECT YOUR DUTIES IN OTHER WAYS. 'HE' WILL STOP AT NOTHING TO *DESTROY* ME! ENSURE EVERYTHING IS LOCKED UP BELOW.

WHO IS 'HE'? WHO DO YOU FEAR?

'HIM'!

WE WENT DOWN INTO THE HOLD, WHERE THE HALF-DEAD — MEN WHO HAD DIED BUT WERE TRAPPED BETWEEN THE PLANES — WERE KEPT...

HUNTERS WOULD BRING THEM IN FROM THE SOURLANDS AND SELL THEM TO MERCHANTS FOR SHIPMENT NORTH...

WHERE THEY WOULD BE USED BY WARRING TRIBES AS 'BATTLE-FODDER'.

NO! IN LUG'S NAME, IT CANNOT BE!

MY OLD FRIENDS... KILLER STYR! SHAVRAN THE SURLY! AND, BY THE LOOK OF THAT ARMOUR, BRES BLOODSPEAR!

DON'T YOU REMEMBER ME...? SLAINE OF THE SESSAIR. WE WERE MERCENARIES TOGETHER! HEY, SHARVAN YOU OLD BEAR!

IT'S NO USE, SLAINE! HE DOESN'T KNOW YOU ANYMORE...

HE'S JOINED THE HALF-DEAD!

MY COMRADES DESERVED BETTER THAN THIS. ONCE THEY WERE PROUD WARRIORS... NOW THEY'RE GHOULS TRAPPED IN TIME!

ON DECK...

ASSASSIN! IF I HADN'T TURNED ROUND, THAT BARREL WOULD HAVE KILLED ME!

AN ACCIDENT, LORD. IT SLIPPED FROM MY GRASP!

MAYBE YOU *THOUGHT* IT WAS AN ACCIDENT, BUT I KNOW IT WAS 'HIM'! SLÁINE, YOU SHOULD HAVE BEEN HERE TO PROTECT ME. 'HE' IS OUT TO GET ME!

BUT I'LL SHOW 'HIM'! STRIP THIS MAN AND TIE HIM TO THE MAST!

THE DRUNE LORD RAISED HIS HAND AND MADE MYSTIC OGHAM SIGNS...

THE UNFORTUNATE SKYFARER HAD A CLEAR VIEW OF HIS IMPENDING FATE... A CLOUD OF BLACK SPECKS FLYING TOWARDS HIM...

AS THEY DREW CLOSER, HE SAW THEY WERE CROWS.

NOTHING ELSE HAPPENED THAT DAY.

BUT, NEXT MORNING, SWOLLEN BLACK CLOUDS APPEARED, HIDING THE SUN.

A HOWLING GALE OVERTOOK US...

AND HURLED THE CLOUD CURRAGH DOWNWARD...

I'VE NEVER KNOWN SUCH A FURY! I THOUGHT YOU DRUNES COULD CONTROL THE ELEMENTS?

'HE' IS TRYING TO DESTROY ME!

WHO IS 'HE'? ANSWER ME, THROT, OR —

THE STONE IS WEAKENING —

WE MUST SACRIFICE A BULL!

SACRIFICIAL BULLS WERE KEPT ON BOARD LARGE SHIPS. IN TIMES OF DANGER, THEIR BLOOD COULD BOOST THE POWER OF THE WEIRD STONE WHICH KEPT A SHIP ALOFT. BUT, TERRIFIED BY THE STORM, THE BULLS BROKE OUT OF THEIR PEN...

AND STAMPEDED ACROSS THE DECK...

AAAAAH!

I KNOW WHO'S AFTER HIM, LORD! A DRUNE FEARS NO-ONE — BUT ANOTHER DRUNE!

YOUR DWARF IS RIGHT. BY TRAVELLING NORTH I AM DEFYING THE LORD WEIRD, SLOUGH FEG!

THAT'S WHY I CHOSE YOU AS MY BODYGUARD! BECAUSE YOU OUTWITTED HIM AT DRUNEMETON!

SO, WE'RE CAUGHT IN A BATTLE OF SORCERORS!

FIRST THINGS FIRST, LORD. HERE COME THE BULLS!

SAVE ME, SLÁINE!

NEXT PROG: SLÁINE THE BEAST TAMER.

Sláine

SLÁINE RELUCTANTLY AGREED TO PROTECT THE SINISTER DRUNE LORD, SLOUGH THROT. THEN, AS WE TRAVELLED NORTH BY CLOUD CURRAGH, WE DISCOVERED HE WAS A RENEGADE, WANTED BY THE LORD WEIRD, SLOUGH FEG. A BATTLE OF SORCERY FOLLOWED...

THE SHIP IS SINKING! UNLESS THE WEIRD STONE TASTES BLOOD, WE ARE LOST!

SLÁINE WRESTLED ONE OF THE ESCAPED CREATURES TO THE DECK...

SC2 21
PAT MILLS
ART
MIKE McMAHON
LETTERING
TOM FRAME

THE REST SMASHED THROUGH THE GUNWHALES CARRYING PASSENGERS AND CREW WITH THEM...

...GORED ON THEIR HORNS.

SLÁINE DRAGGED HIS BEAST BACK TO THE POUND —

HURRY! THE MOUNTAIN PEAKS ARE BELOW US!

THE SACRIFICE WAS MADE.

JUGS WERE FILLED TO BRIMMING WITH THE BULL'S BLOOD.

THEN POURED OVER THE SHIP'S *WEIRD STONE*...

THE STRANGE ROCK DRANK THE WARM LIQUID GREEDILY...

AND BEGAN GLOWING AGAIN, THRUSTING THE SHIP UPWARDS...

WHILE, AT THE SAME TIME, THE FURY OF THE STORM ABATED.

I HAVE TRIUMPHED OVER SLOUGH FEG! MY MAGIC IS GREATER THAN HIS!

YOU DIDN'T SAVE US! SLÁINE KILLED THE BULL!

LISTEN, YOU STINKARD, WHEN I AGREED TO BE YOUR BATTLE-SMITER, YOU DIDN'T TELL ME YOU'D FALLEN OUT WITH YOUR LEADER! FEG WON'T REST UNTIL YOU'RE DEAD...

...AND MAYBE I SHOULD SAVE HIM THE TROUBLE!

YES, GO ON! KILL HIM! WHILE HE LIVES WE'RE IN DANGER!

BUT YOU GAVE YOUR WORD...THE WORD OF A SESSAIR WARRIOR!

BREAKING MY WORD TO A DRUNE IS NO HARDSHIP.

ANYWAY, SLÁINE GOT KICKED OUT OF HIS TRIBE — AFTER THAT TROUBLE WITH NIAMH. SEE, SHE WAS THE KING'S CHOSEN ONE, AND HE...

ALL RIGHT, DWARF, THAT'S ENOUGH!

NOW TELL ME WHY FEG WANTS YOU DEAD...

...OR I'LL DRIVE A HOLE THROUGH YOUR BODY A BIRD CAN FLY THROUGH!

IT MIGHT HAVE GONE BADLY FOR THE PRIEST-KING, BUT AT THAT MOMENT...

SKYBLADES!

THE VESSELS OF THE NORSEMEN WHO PLUNDERED THE SKY-WAYS!

HOW DID THEY FIND US? WE'VE BEEN BLOWN OFF THE USUAL ROUTE.

THE LORD WEIRD MUST HAVE GUIDED THEIR SAILS! YOUR EXPLANATION MUST LIE QUIET FOR NOW, SLOUGH THROT!

THE SKYBLADES SWEPT DOWN. MOST OF THEIR CREWS WERE *BERSERKERS*, FOLLOWERS OF THE GOD VODEN, MEN OF SUPERHUMAN STRENGTH.

THEY WERE HOWLING HORRIBLY, CUTTING AT THEMSELVES, AND BITING THEIR SHIELDS!

IN THE *FIRST SHIP* WAS THORGRIM IRONJAW, HADRIC HISSING BLADE AND BORK THE BRUTAL...

A FAT PRIZE TO TAKE BACK TO MIDGARD! PREPARE BOARDING BASKETS!

IN THE *SECOND* SHIP WERE HENGIST THE STRONG BUT STINGY, RALF RAZORAXE AND HOGNI THE NOT-NORMAL...

REMEMBER, MEN, ALL THE *LOOT* BELONGS TO *ME!* YOU GET YOUR WAGES!

IN THE *THIRD* SHIP WERE SKULD THE DEMENTED, EIRIK CHISELSPEAR AND HERG THE HARD...

THESE WERE THE MEN WHO TORE OUT THROATS WITH THEIR TEETH AND WRESTLED WITH TREES OR BOULDERS IF NO ENEMY WAS AVAILABLE!

THE FIRST SKYBLADE LOWERED ITS BOARDING BASKETS...

GATHER THE ACORN * CROP FOR LORD VODEN!

FOR VODEN! FOR VODEN!

* ACORNS—HEADS.

MORE BERSERKERS SLID DOWN GRAPPLING LINES.

AHOI! AHOI!

AH-A A A AAAAAA

AS SLÁINE WINCHED THE HALF-DEAD UP FROM THE HOLD, THE WEIRDSTONE ON DECK STIRRED THEM INTO GHASTLY LIFE —

NO! THOSE SLAVES BELONG TO ME!

FORGET YOUR PROFITS, MERCHANT — OR YOU'LL TASTE MY FIST!

KILLER STYR, SHARVAN THE SURLY, BRES BLOODSPEAR... I GIVE YOU ONE LAST CHANCE TO FIGHT TOGETHER!

MAY LUG GUIDE YOUR AXES!

SLÁINE TIPPED THE WOODEN CAGE OVER THE SIDE...

... SMASHING IT OPEN ON THE SKYBLADE'S DECK!

HI! HI! HI!

THE BERSERKERS THEY FACED WERE SAVAGE WARRIORS... BUT NOTHING COULD MATCH THE DEMONIC FURY OF THESE CREATURES FROM BEYOND THE GRAVE!

THE SHIP VEERED OUT OF CONTROL AND CRASHED!

NEXT PROG: CHARIOTS ON FIRE!

LIKE MOST TRIBES OF THE EARTH GODDESS, THE SESSAIR WERE HEAD-HUNTERS. ENEMY BRAINBALLS WERE GREATLY PRIZED AS TROPHIES AND DRINKING VESSELS.

BUT AS SLÁINE LOOKED DOWN IN TRIUMPH...

UUUH...

UKKO!

I SAVED YOUR LIFE, SLÁINE! I SAVED YOUR LIFE! NEVER FORGET!

H'MMPH!

BUT THE POWER WAS GREATER THAN THE DRUNE LORD COULD CONTROL.

THE DECK OF OUR SHIP WAS PELTED WITH RED-HOT ROCKS...

I TOLD YOU THIS WOULD HAPPEN, SLÁINE...

WE'RE ALL GOING TO DIE.

THE SHIP'S TURNING OVER!

YOU'RE MY BATTLE-SMITER, SLÁINE...

...SAVE ME!

SLÁINE SWUNG THE TILLER, TRYING TO RIGHT THE STRICKEN VESSEL.

THERE WERE ONLY FOUR SURVIVORS...

TRUST SLOUGH THROT TO ESCAPE UNHARMED.

WE CONTINUED THE JOURNEY ON FOOT...

THAT'S THE LAST TIME I TRAVEL BY SKY CHARIOT. WHERE ARE WE?

HOW SHOULD I KNOW. HURRY UP, DWARF!

I'M TIRED, SLAINE! CAN I RIDE ON YOUR BACK?

NO.

THAT'S BETTER...! AT LEAST NOTHING ELSE BAD CAN BEFALL US.

I'M NOT SO SURE. REMEMBER, THE LORD WEIRD TRIED TO KILL SLOUGH THROT...

IT'S MY BELIEF HE'LL TRY AGAIN!

LET HIM! WE DON'T WANT TO GET MIXED UP IN ANY MORE SORCERY!

BUT AS WE PROGRESSED ALONG OUR PATH. . .

IN THE DARK FOREST, MANY EYES WERE WATCHING. . .

AND WAITING!

IT WAS THE MERCHANT WHO NOTICED IT FIRST. . .

THERE'S SOMETHING UNCANNY ABOUT THIS PLACE. . .

IT'S SO QUIET. . .

AYE!

NOT EVEN THE LEAVES RUSTLE!

THEN, FROM THE UNDERGROWTH, SOMETHING HURLED ITSELF AT SLOUGH THROT...

A BOAR!

SLÁINE!

SAVE ME!

SLÁINE HURLED HIS AXE...

HREEEEE

IT'S TURNED ON HIM!

I CAN'T LOOK!

THIS ROCK CAN ALSO MARK YOUR GRAVE!

SO WHY AREN'T YOU LOOKING FORWARD TO THIS DISASTER LIKE YOUR MASTER?

I...

I'LL TELL YOU WHY, UKKO... BECAUSE HE ENJOYS POWER TOO MUCH.

THE POWER THAT WILL DIE WHEN THE RAGNORAK COMES. THE POWER THAT, USED FOR EVIL, ROTS AND DECAYS.

I KNOW WHAT YOU MEAN... HE SMELLS LIKE A CHICKEN-HOUSE!

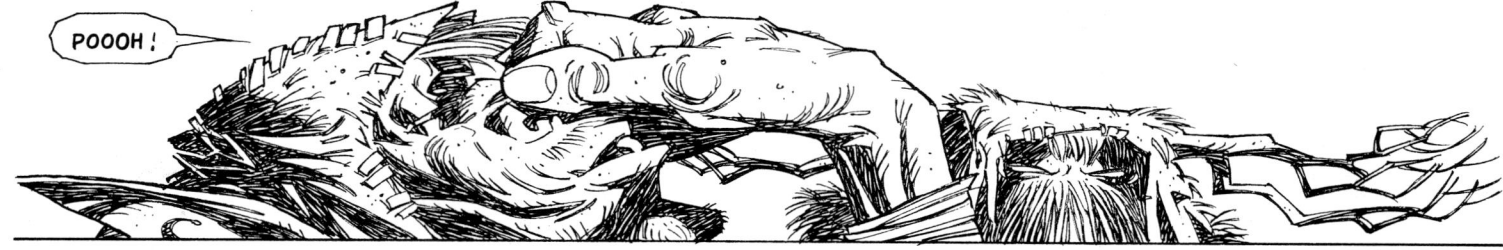

POOOH!

MY 'MYSTIC AURA' IS A SMALL PRICE TO PAY FOR WHAT I HAVE ACHIEVED.

I CAME NORTH TO SHOW THESE PLANS TO YOUR DRUIDS.

I'LL PAY YOU WELL TO ESCORT ME THE REST OF THE WAY.

THE SORCERER DID NOT NOTICE THE WORMS PUSHING UP THROUGH THE GROUND.

I'M NOT INTERESTED IN YOUR GOLD.

I AM!

THEN, THE BEASTS BEGAN TO MOVE OFF...

THAT WAS A CLOSE ONE!

SLÁINE?

WAIT FOR ME!

AND SO WE LEFT THE FOREST AND CONTINUED OUR OWN JOURNEY...

ONE THING I DON'T UNDERSTAND... HOW DID WE ESCAPE?

MAYBE SOMEONE WAS HELPING US...

BUT WHO...?

...AND WHY?

THE END.

SLÁINE the King

Script: PAT MILLS
Art: GLENN FABRY
Lettering: STEVE POTTER

THE DEATH WINTER HAD FALLEN ON SLÁINE'S WORLD...

...FROM TORY ISLAND, THEIR OUTPOST ON EARTH, A RACE OF MYSTERY AND HORROR — THE FOMORIAN SEA DEMONS — HAD WRITTEN SORROW ON THE LAND OF THE YOUNG...

...THE OFFSPRING OF CHAOS AND OLD NIGHT, THEY HAD SWEPT DOWN THROUGH LOCHLANN, THE REGION OF ICE AND GLOOM, LED BY THEIR KING... *BALOR OF THE EVIL EYE*, WHOSE DEATH-DEALING EYE WITHERED ALL WHO STOOD BEFORE IT!

UGLY AND DEFORMED, SOME FOMORIANS HAD THE HEADS OF GOATS AND BULLS... OTHERS THREE ROWS OF TEETH...

BUT NONE WERE AS GROTESQUE AS QUAGSLIME—THE COLLECTOR OF TAXES...

PLEASE, QUAGSLIME! I NEED MORE TIME TO PAY!

IT WAS QUAGSLIME WHO WAS RESPONSIBLE FOR THE INFAMOUS 'NOSE TAX'...

YOU HAD SEVEN DAYS. AS PAYMENT HAS NOT BEEN RECEIVED, I REGRET I HAVE NO ALTERNATIVE BUT TO...

...CUT OFF YOUR NOSE!

DOH! DOH! LISTEN! I DEEDED TO BUY FUEL! DOT FOR BE—FOR OLD GRANDBOTHER!

H'MM. YES. I SEE THE PROBLEM— AND I'D LIKE TO HELP. NOW HERE'S A SUGGESTION, AND IT'S ONLY A SUGGESTION, MIND...

...BUT WHY DON'T YOU KILL GRANNY?

IT WOULD BE A GREAT SAVING ON YOUR FUEL BILL. HAVE A THINK ABOUT IT, ANYWAY.

MEANWHILE, I'LL HAVE TO REMOVE THIS ORGAN AND YOU'RE REMINDED THAT IF YOU STILL DON'T PAY, SOMETHING ELSE WILL HAVE TO COME OFF...

AAAGGH!

MEANWHILE... SLÁINE'S WOUNDS HAD WHITENED AND HE WAS FINALLY RETURNING TO HIS TRIBE AFTER YEARS OF EXILE—UNAWARE THEY WERE UNDER THE WEBBED FOOT OF THE FOMORIAN...

GOODBYE, SLÁINE.

NEST WAS STAYING ON AT THE ETERNAL FORTRESS TO STUDY HIGH MAGIC...

ALL RIGHT! ALL RIGHT! THAT'S ENOUGH OF THAT! WE'VE A LONG JOURNEY AHEAD OF US!

AS A REWARD FOR HELPING THE EVER-LIVING ONES, MYRDDIN HAD ALLOWED SLÁINE TO TAKE AWAY THE LEGENDARY *CAULDRON OF BLOOD*...

TAKE GOOD CARE OF IT. IT IS THE *MOST SACRED* OF OUR TREASURES AND WILL BE OF MORE USE THAN ANY WEAPON... WHEN YOU BECOME THE SUN KING OF YOUR TRIBE.

"...FOR IT IS THE *CAULDRON OF PLENTY*, CHARGED WITH THE POWER OF THE EARTH GODDESS! IT FEEDS ALL WHO COME BEFORE IT, HEALS THE SICK AND WOUNDED, BRINGS THE DEAD BACK TO LIFE, AND IS THE SATISFACTION OF ALL DESIRES."

IS THAT ALL?

SUCH A VESSEL COULD UNITE THE TRIBES AGAINST THE FOMORIAN INVADERS!

BUT REMEMBER WHAT I HAVE TOLD YOU... HOW YOU MUST *CONTROL* THE CAULDRON'S POWER WHICH CAN BE USED FOR WHITE MAGIC...

...OR *BLACK MAGIC!*

AND SO WE LEFT THE ETERNAL FORTRESS...

MURDACH, TOO, WAS STAYING BEHIND, HOPING TO PERSUADE MYRDDIN TO RETURN HIM TO HIS OWN TIME — ALTHOUGH THE MAGUS HAD SAID THIS WAS IMPOSSIBLE...

USING ITS FIERY BREATH TO GAIN HEIGHT, SOARING ON THE THERMALS, THE KNUCKER FLEW HIGH OVER SNOWDONIA...

SO YOU'LL BE SEEING *NIAMH* AT LAST... YOUR LONG-LOST LOVE?

NIAMH, IN CASE YOU'VE FORGOTTEN (BECAUSE SLÁINE CERTAINLY HAD), WAS THE GIRL HE HAD DISHONOURED — CAUSING HIM TO BE BANISHED FROM HIS TRIBE...

AYE. HER YEARS OF WAITING FOR ME ARE OVER. WE'LL BE TOGETHER AND SHE'LL SHARE MY STALL IN THE GREAT ROUND HALL OF HEROES.

I'M GLAD TO HEAR ONE OF YOU HAS BEEN WAITING. YOU CERTAINLY HAVEN'T!

SILENCE, DWARF — OR YOU WILL FEEL MY WRATHFUL RIGHT HAND...

...AND STOP THAT SCRATCHING! I'VE TOLD YOU BEFORE IT'S TIME YOU HAD YOUR YEARLY BATH!

I'M NOT *SCRATCHING!*

FUNNY, THOUGH... I HEARD IT TOO...

I THOUGHT IT WAS COMING FROM THE CAULDRON...

YOU DIRTY LITTLE DWARF! COME ON — IT'S TIME WE WERE MOVING.

LISTEN! CAN YOU HEAR SOMETHING ...MOANING?

PROBABLY THE KNUCKER SUCKING THE MARROW OUT OF THE ANTLERS... THAT'S HIS FAVOURITE BIT.

PROBABLY. ANYWAY, I WAS TALKING TO MURDACH AND HE RECKONS THAT BIT ABOUT SINFUL DESIRES WAS ADDED LATER, IN CHRISTIAN TIMES.

ORIGINALLY, THEY USED TO SAY THE CAULDRON "WILL NOT COOK THE FOOD OF A COWARD".

WHO CAN UNDERSTAND THE WHIMS OF THE GODS? ALL I KNOW IS IT'S AN ENTRANCE TO THE INNER EL WORLDS OF GODS AND DEMONS...

...POWERFUL FORCES OF LIGHT AND DARKNESS THAT CAN ERUPT AT ANY TIME.

WHAT IS IT?

AVAGDDU... THE SON OF THE EARTH GODDESS! SHE HAD THREE CHILDREN... ONE WAS THE UGLIEST, MOST STUPID AND EVIL CREATURE THAT EVER EXISTED...

AVAGDDU! THE DARK SIDE OF EARTH POWER!

HE'S GONE!

FOR NOW. HE SMELT THE BLOOD. HE'LL WANT FEEDING ...AND SOON.

NEXT TIME THE SIGN OF LIGHT WON'T BE ENOUGH TO STOP HIM.

OH, WELL... THERE'S USUALLY NO SHORTAGE OF BLOOD WHEN YOU'RE AROUND.

MEANWHILE... IN MURIAS—CAPITAL OF SLAINE'S TRIBE—NIAMH HAD GONE TO SEE THE KING...

RAGALL, YOUR PEOPLE ARE STARVING! MY OWN SON WON'T SEE HIS SIXTH SPRING! HOW CAN WE PAY THE FOMORIAN TAXES WHEN OUR CROPS WON'T GROW? IT—IT'S MADNESS!

NOW, NIAMH, I THINK WE SHOULD LOWER THE TEMPERATURE A LITTLE... AFTER ALL, *QUAGSLIME*, THE COLLECTOR OF TAXES, IS PRESENT...

HOW MUCH LOWER? WE'RE ALREADY FREEZING TO DEATH!

WE FOMORIANS LIKE TO HELP IN CASES OF SPECIAL HARDSHIP SUCH AS THIS. WE'RE NOT CRUEL AND HEARTLESS TYRANTS, YOU KNOW... WE TRY TO BE AS *POSITIVE* AND *CONSTRUCTIVE* AS WE CAN. TELL ME, NIAMH...

...HAVE YOU CONSIDERED EATING YOUR SON?

I DON'T SPEAK TO FISH.

OUR FEMALES OFTEN EAT THEIR YOUNG.

ER... HUMANS ARE A LITTLE DIFFERENT, QUAGSLIME. WHAT ABOUT THE BOY'S FATHER, NIAMH? COULDN'T HE HELP?

DON'T EVEN MENTION HIS NAME!

NEXT TO THE FISH, HE'S THE ONE I HATE MOST IN ALL THE WORLD!

Next: BLOOD FOR AVAGDDU.

SLÁINE the King

SCRIPT: PAT MILLS
ART: GLENN FABRY
LETTERING: STEVE POTTER

YOU'VE CHANGED, RAGALL—EVER SINCE YOU MARRIED...

...HER.

WE KNOW NOTHING ABOUT HER! WHERE SHE CAME FROM... WHO SHE IS...

BUT MEGRIM TOLD US—A PRINCESS OF THE SOUTHERN TRIBES WHO FLED THE TYRANNY OF THE DRUNE LORDS.

...NOR IF MEGRIM IS HER REAL NAME!

SHE'S PUT A GLAMOUR* ON YOU!

*GLAMOUR—AN ENCHANTMENT.

OF COURSE I HAVE...

WOULDN'T ANY YOUNG WIFE?

THESE ARE TROUBLED TIMES, NIAMH... I INVITED THE FOMORIANS TO ESTABLISH MILITARY BASES ON OUR SOIL SO THEY COULD PROTECT US.

PROTECT US FROM WHAT, IN LUG'S NAME?

FROM HAVING YOUR GIZZARD RIPPED OUT, YOUR ENTRAILS WRAPPED ROUND A TREE, AND DYING IN AGONY IN NOT ONE OR TWO DAYS, BUT A WHOLE *WEEK*.

NIAMH DOESN'T MEAN TO COMPLAIN, QUAGSLIME. YOU KNOW HOW HOT-TEMPERED WE CELTS ARE...

AND YOU KNOW HOW COLD-BLOODED WE FOMORIANS ARE...

POOR NIAMH... I UNDERSTAND... IT CAN'T BE EASY FOR YOU, BRINGING UP A SON ALONE...

DON'T PATRONISE ME, YOU—!

MAY THE SACRED EARTH MOTHER PROTECT US...

...LOOK AT HER TRUE FORM, RAGALL! SHE'S A CREATURE FROM THE EL WORLDS!

CAN'T YOU SEE, RAGALL? CAN'T YOU SEE?

ALL I SEE IS A HYSTERICAL WOMAN... FINISH HER, MEGRIM. IT IS YOUR RIGHT.

NO... I CAN'T BRING MYSELF TO.

NOW YOU KNOW HOW KIND AND GENTLE MY WIFE IS. NOW YOU KNOW WHY I LOVE HER. FOR YOUR WICKED ACCUSATIONS, YOU MUST BE BANISHED FROM THIS TRIBE AS YOUR LOVER ONCE WAS—NEVER TO RETURN!

There were four worlds inside the earth... at right angles to our own, and thus known as 'L' or EL worlds...

World of Dev-els and Ang-els **1**	World of the Elder Gods **2**
3 World of elemental creatures like Elves and Goblins	**4** World of the dead

Through these natural forces of light and darkness, a race of star beings— the Cythrons— had sought to control the earth.

SLÁINE the King

SCRIPT:
PAT MILLS
ART:
FABRY/WILLIAMS
LETTERING:
STEVE POTTER

"From an old and evil custom the Celts always carry an axe in their hand as if it were a staff. Wherever they go, they drag it along with them. In this way, if they have a feeling for evil, they can more quickly give it effect..."

KISS MY AXE!

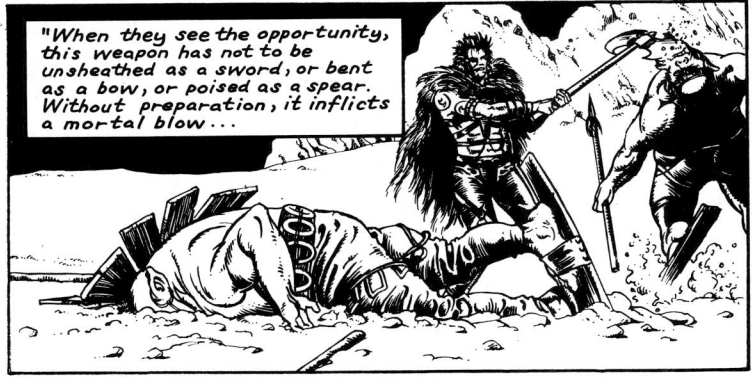

"When they see the opportunity, this weapon has not to be unsheathed as a sword, or bent as a bow, or poised as a spear. Without preparation, it inflicts a mortal blow..."

"At hand, or rather, in the hand and ever ready, is that which is enough to cause death."
Ancient Chronicle

ANOTHER FOR AVAGDDU!

BUT AVAGDDU, DISEASED SON OF THE EARTH GODDESS, COULD NOT WAIT...

BEFORE THE FOMORIANS COULD ALL BE KILLED AND THEIR BLOOD POURED INTO THE CAULDRON, THE CREATURE LEAPT OUT...

GRABBED TWO SEA DEMONS AND DRAGGED THEM SCREAMING...

SPLAT!

...DOWN INTO HIS INNER WORLD...

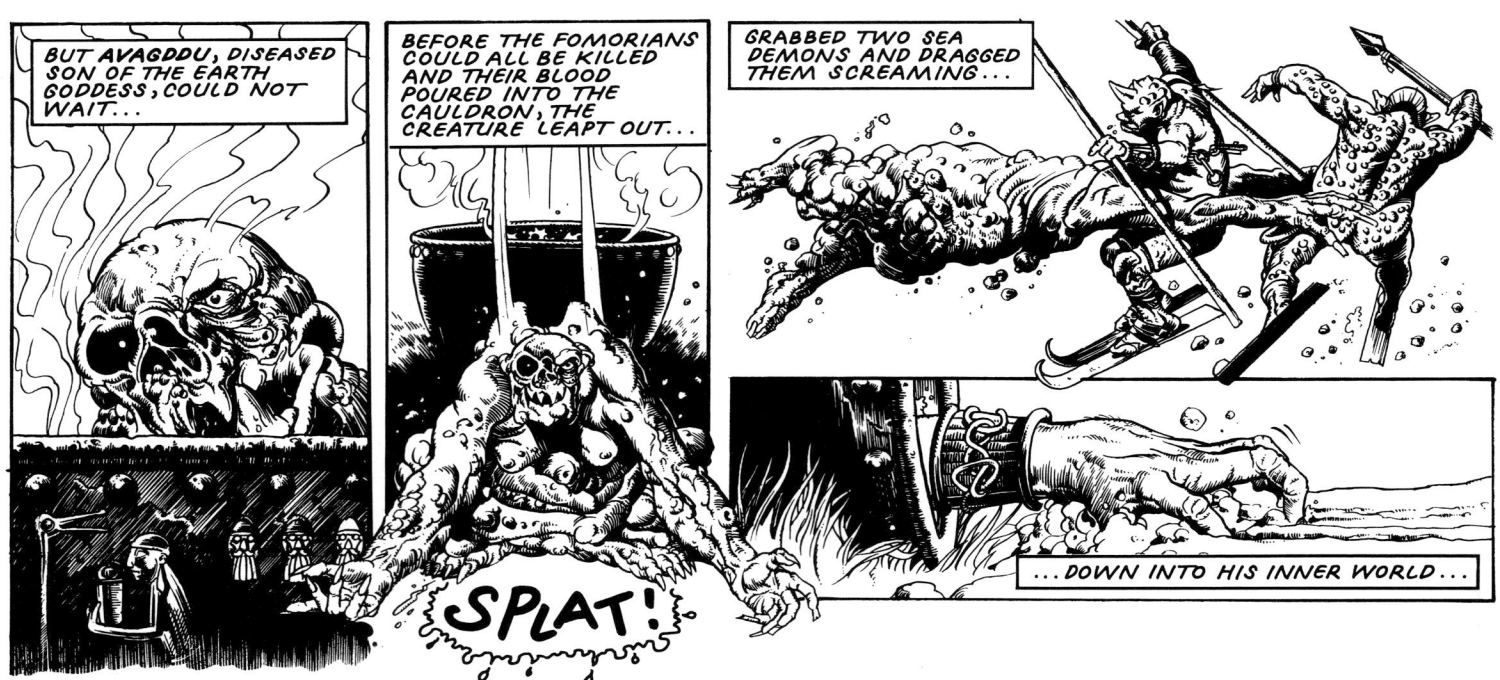

...WHERE HE QUENCHED HIS THIRST.

WE COULD HEAR HIS INSANE GIGGLES AS HE DRANK THEIR BLOOD, IN THE MISTAKEN BELIEF IT WOULD HALT HIS EVERLASTING DECAY...

MIND YOU, WITH A MOTHER LIKE DANU THE EARTH GODDESS, I'M NOT SURPRISED HE'S OFF HIS HEAD!

SEVEN FOMORIANS LAY STARK DEAD. SLÁINE DIDN'T THINK IT TOO MANY.

COME ON —WE SHOULD REACH MY TRIBE BY STARFALL.

YOU SHOULD BE PROUD TO GIVE YOUR LIFE TO THE PRIESTHOOD!

COME... *GERG OF THE THREE FINGERS* WILL DRIVE YOU AS FAR AS GORIAS.

AYE. THE WOODS ARE NO PLACE FOR A WOMAN AND CHILD ALONE.

DON'T WANT TO GO!

YOU'LL DO WHAT YOU'RE TOLD AND LIKE IT, MY LAD!

I'M AFRAID HIS FATHER WOULD HAVE PREFERRED HIM TO BE A WARRIOR.

I DON'T CARE! I *HATE* HIS FATHER!

YOU DIDN'T HATE *SLÁINE* ONCE, NIAMH...

I... I WAS YOUNG THEN, AND FOOLISH...

LOVE AND HATE... WHAT ARE THEY BUT OPPOSITE SIDES OF THE SAME LEAF? WHEN THE WIND OF FATE BLOWS, THE LEAF MAY TURN AND—

GERG?

YES, NIAMH?

SHUT UP.

YES, NIAMH.

LOOK AT HER GLOATING! EVERY TIME I SEE THAT COW, MY GORGE RISES.

DOESN'T YOURS?

WELL... NOT EXACTLY, NIAMH...

YOU'RE TAKEN IN BY HER FAIRNESS OF FORM, LIKE THE OTHERS. CAN'T YOU SEE WHAT SHE'S LIKE UNDERNEATH?

NO. WHAT'S SHE LIKE?

NIGHT-SOIL! EVIL THROUGH AND THROUGH! SHE'LL DESTROY OUR TRIBE!

DON'T BE SILLY. SHE'S ONLY SEVENTEEN — A SLIP OF A GIRL.

SEVENTEEN GOING ON FORTY!

WHAT SHE KNOWS, SOME WOULD TAKE A LIFETIME DISCOVERING...

WHAT WILL YOU DO WHEN THE BOY'S GONE?

JOIN THE FREE TRIBES—AS YOU SHOULD, GERG.

NO... I'M SLÁINE'S CHARIOTEER... I COULDN'T DRIVE FOR ANYONE ELSE.

Next: THE REUNION!

"Nearly all the Celts are terrifying from the sternness of their eyes, very quarrelsome and with great pride and insolence... But a whole troop of foreigners could not withstand one if he called his **wife** to his assistance...

"She is usually very strong and with blue eyes... especially when, swelling her neck, gnashing her teeth and brandishing her sallow arms...

"...she begins to strike blows mingled with kicks, as if they were so many missiles sent from the string of a catapult."
Ancient description of Celtic women.

SOMEONE IN TROUBLE DOWN THERE! WE MUST HELP THEM!

WHY?

NIAMH, WHAT'S WRONG? WHAT'S CHANGED BETWEEN US?

SEE FOR YOURSELF...

MY SON?!

BUT HE SHOULD BRING US CLOSER. I DON'T UNDERSTAND.

YOU REALLY DON'T, DO YOU? DESPITE WHAT HAPPENED!

WHAT EXACTLY DID HAPPEN, DEAR? YOU SEE, I'VE ONLY HEARD HIS VERSION.

ABOUT HOW I WAS THE KING'S 'CHOSEN ONE'? OH, YES, THAT'S TRUE... I WAS SELECTED AS A CHILD, BECAUSE MY LOOKS PLEASED HIM...

"...AND KEPT A PRISONER IN A HUT AWAY FROM THE REST OF THE TRIBE, UNTIL I WAS OLD ENOUGH TO MARRY..."

"OH, THE KING WAS VERY KIND... BUT I WAS HIS PROPERTY. I HAD TO WEAR MY HAIR AND DRESS THE WAY HE LIKED IT...

"WARRIORS WERE FORBIDDEN TO GO NEAR THE HUT ON PAIN OF TORTURE AND DEATH...

"BUT, OF COURSE, THAT DIDN'T STOP SLÁINE...

"AND... FOR A LITTLE WHILE... I WAS FREE...

"UNTIL WE WERE DISCOVERED TOGETHER..."

WAIT TILL THE KING HEARS ABOUT THIS!

YOU'RE DEAD, BOY!

SLÁINE ESCAPED THE KING'S WRATH, BUT I DIDN'T. WHEN HE KNEW I WAS GOING TO HAVE KAI, HE PLANNED A CRUEL REVENGE...

Next: NIAMH'S PUNISHMENT!

"WHEN MY TIME CAME, THE KING ORDERED THAT I GO THROUGH IT ALONE ...TO PUNISH ME...

"...ALTHOUGH I KNEW NOTHING.

"I TOLD MYSELF THAT NIGHT... NEVER FORGET THIS!"

"NEVER FORGET THIS!"

NEVER!

"BUT I WAS NOT ALONE... I CALLED ON THE GREAT EARTH GODDESS— MOTHER OF ALL CREATURES —AND SHE ANSWERED ME... SHE GAVE ME THE COURAGE AND STRENGTH I NEEDED...

"AFTERWARDS, I WASN'T ALLOWED TO FOSTER HIM IN THE TRADITIONAL WAY, OR TURN TO OTHER WOMEN FOR HELP. I HAD TO BRING KAI UP IN THAT HUT ON MY OWN...

"...SO NO-ONE COULD SEE HOW I'D MADE A FOOL OF THE KING."

WHILE YOU WERE FREE TO ROAM THE LAND OF THE YOUNG, I WAS A PRISONER AGAIN.

I DIDN'T KNOW. IF I HAD, I'D HAVE COME BACK SOONER.

WE GOT A BIT DELAYED DOING GREAT DEEDS.

YES, MY GUARDS TOLD ME ABOUT YOUR *GREAT DEEDS*. YOUR ADVENTURES TOGETHER HAVE BECOME LEGENDS...

REALLY? WELL, I SUPPOSE I MUST TAKE THE CREDIT THERE. YOU SEE, WHEN A YOUNG MAN'S ONLY SIXTEEN—LIKE SLÁINE WAS—IT'S VERY EASY TO FALL IN WITH DISHONEST PEOPLE. THEY NEED A GOOD INFLUENCE...

SOMEONE TO KEEP THEM ON THE STRAIGHT AND NARROW, AWAY FROM TEMPTATION AND BAD WOMEN...

...LUCKILY, SLÁINE MET ME.

OH, YES. MANY'S THE TIME I'D SAY, "SLÁINE, MY BOY"... I WAS LIKE A FATHER FIGURE TO HIM, YOU SEE... "LEAVE THAT GOLD ALONE! YOU MUSTN'T TAKE THINGS THAT DON'T BELONG TO YOU, SON."

ADMIRABLE.

SO WHAT ABOUT THE TIME THE TWO OF YOU BOUGHT A PRISON, SO YOU COULD TAKE BRIBES FROM THE PRISONERS TO LET THEM ESCAPE?

AH... WELL...

OR WHEN YOU SUGGESTED HE EXHIBIT HIMSELF AS A FAIRGROUND FREAK?

"ABUSING THE POWERS GIVEN HIM BY THE GODDESS TO LIFT A HORSE OFF THE GROUND WITH HIS THIGHS.'"

ROLL UP! ROLL UP! SEE THE WARPED MAN IN ACTION!

AND FOUND COMFORT IN THE ARMS OF SOME SPECKLED-FACE TROLLOP CALLED HEN OR CHICKEN OR SOMETHING.

ER... NEST, ACTUALLY.

WHILST YOU EXPECT *ME* TO HAVE REMAINED FAITHFUL TO *YOU* ALL THESE YEARS, AND BE WAITING FOR YOU—PURE AS THE DRIVEN SNOW—WHILE *YOU'VE* BEEN GOING ROUND LIKE A *RAMPANT LION!*

YES, SHE'S GOT A POINT, SLÁINE.

WHEN THE KING DIED AND I WAS FREED, I SWORE I'D NEVER RELY ON ANY-ONE AGAIN... LEAST OF ALL ON YOU...

...AND I OFFERED KAI TO THE EARTH GODDESS IN THANKSGIVING.

YOU'RE TAKING HIM TO MY OLD MILITARY TRAINING SCHOOL AT ALBA? EXCELLENT!

NO. THE DRUID SEMINARY AT DURRINGTON.

MY SON... A DRUID!

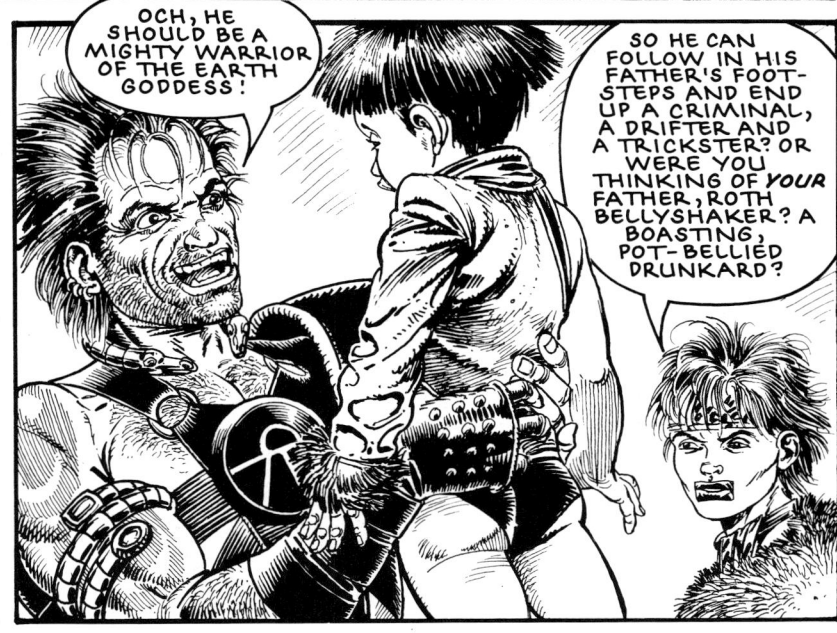

OCH, HE SHOULD BE A MIGHTY WARRIOR OF THE EARTH GODDESS!

SO HE CAN FOLLOW IN HIS FATHER'S FOOT-STEPS AND END UP A CRIMINAL, A DRIFTER AND A TRICKSTER? OR WERE YOU THINKING OF *YOUR* FATHER, ROTH BELLYSHAKER? A BOASTING, POT-BELLIED DRUNKARD?

MY FATHER IS DEAD.

SO IS KAI'S.

GOODBYE, SLÁINE.

Next: MEGRIM REVEALED.

SLÁINE the KING

SCRIPT: PAT MILLS
ART: GLENN FABRY
LETTERING: STEVE POTTER

FOOD!

FOOD!

I'M SORRY, I'D LIKE TO HELP YOU — BUT I HAVE TO BE CRUEL TO BE KIND. IT'S TIME YOU ALL LEARNED TO STAND ON YOUR OWN TWO FEET.

THOSE OF YOU WHO STILL *HAVE* FEET.

POOR WRETCHES. I ONLY HOPE THE NEW KING WILL BRING THE SUN BACK INTO THEIR LIVES.

WHAT NEW KING?

I'M SORRY, MEGRIM — I MEANT TO TELL YOU BEFORE. IT'S BEEN AGREED... I'M TO GO INTO THE EARTH TOMORROW.

BUT A SACRED KING RULES FOR SEVEN YEARS BEFORE HE'S PUT TO DEATH!

NOT WHEN HE FAILS HIS PEOPLE.

IF YOU DO NOT DIE WHEN YOUR TIME IS COME THERE IS LOSS OF *EARTH-ROOT!* IT IS THE MOST TERRIBLE CRIME!

BUT YOU CAN DO WHAT YOU LIKE — *YOU'RE THE KING!*

DANU IS CALLING ME NOW... WAITING FOR ME TO MERGE WITH HER...

AND WHAT ABOUT ME? DON'T I COUNT?

I AM MARRIED TO THE EARTH GODDESS BEFORE ANY HUMAN WIFE.

I COULD HAVE BEEN A GODDESS ONCE — THE BRIDE OF THE MOST POWERFUL GOD OF ALL...

YOU MEAN *LUG THE SUN?* OR *HU THE MIGHTY,* WHO IS ABOVE EVEN LUG? I KNOW LITTLE OF YOUR SOUTHERN WAYS.

NO, YOU PATHETIC FOOL! THE GOD WHO FEEDS ON WAR... DISEASE... AND DISASTER...

THE GOD WHO WILL SAVE US BY PUTTING AN END TO THE MISERY OF LIFE ON THIS PLANE...

THE WORM-GOD ...*CROM CRUACH!*

MEGRIM! WHAT ARE YOU SAYING?

HOW I LONGED TO SMELL HIS FETID BREATH... TO FEEL HIS SLIMY FLAGELLUM AROUND ME... TO HEAR THE SCREAMS OF HIS VICTIMS AS HE SUCKED THEIR SOULS...

FREEING THEM FROM THE PAIN OF EXISTENCE!

THEN ONE MAN CHEATED ME OF POWER... YOUR BOYHOOD FRIEND — *SLÁINE!*

I... I DON'T KNOW YOU AT ALL.

NO... MY TRUE NAME IS *MEDB — THE INTOXICATING ONE.* THE DRUNE LORDS SENT ME NORTH TO MARRY A DOLT LIKE YOU AND CAUSE THE DESTRUCTION OF YOUR TRIBE.

A TASK I SHALL COMPLETE AFTER I'VE ENJOYED WATCHING YOU DIE TOMORROW...

AND I AM MADE RULER IN YOUR PLACE.

I'LL KILL YOU FIRST!

YOU WON'T! YOU'LL DO WHAT I WANT. YOU CAN'T HELP YOURSELF.

A TRICKLE OF BLOOD... POINTING TO MEGRIM!

AN OMEN! SHE SHALL RULE US NOW!

MEANWHILE... WE HAD ARRIVED IN MURIAS...

SO THIS IS YOUR HOME-CITY, SLÁINE. I SEE THEY LEAVE THEIR DOORS UN-LOCKED... THAT'S VERY TRUSTWORTHY.

OF COURSE, UKKO. WHAT SORT OF PERSON WOULD STEAL FROM HIS NEIGHBOUR?

WHAT'S GOING ON OVER THERE?

I PROMISE, AS YOUR QUEEN, I SHALL LEAD THIS TRIBE TO ITS TRUE DESTINY...

WAIT, GIRL! THE BLOOD'S CHANGING DIRECTION...

IT'S LEADING TO...

SLÁINE!

IT IS A SIGN FROM THE EARTH GODDESS... SLÁINE IS YOUR NEW KING!

Next: FUNERAL GAMES.

Sláine the King

SCRIPT:
PAT MILLS
ART:
GLENN FABRY
LETTERING:
STEVE POTTER

I'M DYING, SLÁINE.

YOU ARE.

I'VE BETRAYED MY PEOPLE.

YOU HAVE.

YOU MUST MAKE THE SUN SHINE AGAIN.

I WILL.

AS CATHBAD TOOK RAGALL TO THE EARTH WOMB...

A VAGRANT IS TO BE OUR NEW KING? THE SON OF THAT OLD DRUNKARD ROTH BELLYSHAKER?

SLÁINE WAS BAD ENOUGH WHEN HE WAS LITTLE. HE'LL BE WORSE NOW HE'S GROWN.

MONGAN-AXEHEAD—

SLÁINE IS ALSO MY FOSTER SON, MADAD. AND WHEN YOU INSULT MY FAMILY...

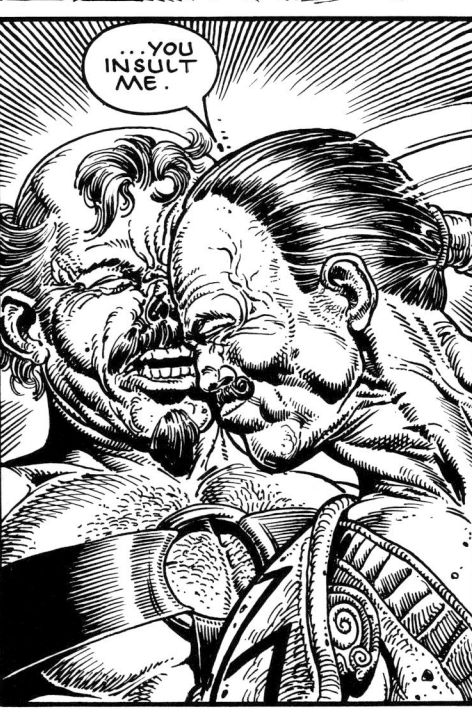

...YOU INSULT ME.

IT WAS THE CUSTOM IN SLÁINE'S TRIBE FOR CHILDREN TO BE BROUGHT UP BY A FOSTER-FATHER...

FOR THAT I'LL SEE YOU JOIN YOUR OTHER SON IN THE EARTH!

YOU? I COULD PUT YOU IN THE *SPITAL HUT* WITH ONE HAND TIED BEHIND MY BACK.

* SPITAL HUT— TRIBAL HOSPITAL.

SAVE YOUR ENERGY FOR THE FORMORS! LET'S STAIN THE EARTH GREY WITH THEIR BRAINS —NOT EACH OTHERS'!

I SEE— ACTING LIKE A KING ALREADY! AND HOW DO YOU PROPOSE WE FIGHT THEM, YOUR HIGHNESS, WHEN WE'VE NO FOOD IN OUR BELLIES?

WITH THE *CAULDRON OF PLENTY!*

SORRY TO TELL YOU THIS BUT WE ALREADY HAVE PLENTY OF CAULDRONS...

IT'S PLENTY TO PUT IN THEM THAT'S THE JOB.

NOT HARD TO SOLVE. THIS IS AN *ENCHANTED* CAULDRON THAT FEEDS ALL WHO COME BEFORE IT!

IT'S CERTAINLY FILLED WITH GOOD ODOURS.

DON'T KNOW IF WE SHOULD EAT ENCHANTED FOOD...WE DON'T KNOW WHERE IT'S COME FROM.

AS LONG AS IT'S FOOD *WHO CARES?* TAKE IT TO THE ROUND HALL!

INSIDE...EVERY WARRIOR WHO STABBED HIS FLESH FORK INTO THE CAULDRON GOT A PIECE OF MEAT ...THERE WAS *PLENTY* FOR MONGAN-AXEHEAD ...PLENTY FOR GURG OF THE THREE FINGERS...

PLENTY FOR MADAD THE QUARRELSOME...

AND NOW, LADIES AND GENTLEMEN, FOR YOUR ENTERTAINMENT I SHOULD LIKE TO TELL YOU ABOUT SOME OF THE *FABULOUS CREATURES* SLÁINE AND I MET ON OUR TRAVELS IN THE SOUTH.

AYE! WE HEARD HE WAS ONE FOR THE LADIES.

NO, NO...NOT *THAT* KIND OF FABULOUS CREATURE! I'M TALKING ABOUT *THE BICORNE*...

A MONSTROUS BEAST— LIKE THE UNICORN —BUT WITH *TWO HORNS.*

THE BICORNE IS ALWAYS HAPPY AND WELL-FED BECAUSE IT DINES ON HEN-PECKED HUSBANDS...

HAAR, HAAR, HAAR.

AND ITS RELATION IS THE COW-LIKE *CHICHEVACHE* THAT ONLY DEVOURS *OBEDIENT WIVES*...

THIS EXPLAINS THE THE BEAST'S *LEAN AND HUNGRY* APPEARANCE.

HAAW, HAAW, HAAW.

YOUR DWARF PLAYS THE PART OF THE COURT JESTER WELL.

AYE. UKKO ALWAYS WAS A *BUFFOON.*

THANK YOU, LADIES AND GENTLEMEN... SHOW YOUR APPRECIATION IN THE USUAL WAY...

THE ROUND HALL REVOLVING WITH WARMTH AND LAUGHTER AGAIN... DRINKING OUT OF MY FAVOURITE SKULL ...IT FEELS GOOD TO BE BACK, MONGAN.

BUT OUTSIDE...

YOU KNOW WHAT TO DO... GIVE SLÁINE *THE WELCOME HOME* HE DESERVES!

Next: THE WARPING!

THE SIGHT OF THE PEOPLE HE LOVED...
THE GIRLS HE'D GROWN UP WITH...
HUMILIATED...COWERING IN FEAR
FROM THESE SEA CREATURES...
BROUGHT ON SLÁINE'S WARP SPASM...

IT WAS A PARTICULARLY FINE WARP SPASM!

PLEASANT TO ME THE WHISTLE OF MY THIRST-MADDENED AXE...

THE POWER OF THE EARTH GODDESS SURGED THROUGH HIM...

AND THOSE OF US WHO HAVE MADE A SPECIAL STUDY OF SLÁINE'S MAGICAL FURIES I THINK WOULD AGREE...

...AS IT SLAKES ITSELF IN FOMORIAN BLOOD!

JOIN ME IN THE HEAD-HARVEST! DRIVE THE FISH-MEN BACK TO THEIR SUBMARINE PALACES!

SLÁINE'S FRENZY AROUSED THE WARRIORS FROM THEIR STRANGE LETHARGY...

THE AURA OF THE SUN IS AROUND HIM! HE SHINES RED! HE SHINES VERY RED!

HE HAS GIVEN US ALL NEW HEARTS! GO TO WORK WITH YOUR BLADES!

TRULY IT IS SAID...

EVERY WEAPON HAS ITS DEMON!

NO FOMORS ESCAPED...AFTER-WARDS— THEY ROLLED SLAINE IN THE SNOW TO COOL HIS HERO-HEAT...

AS CLOSE-BY, MEDB WATCHED...

IT IS ONLY THE BEGINNING, SLAINE...WHERE BRUTE FORCE FAILED, SORCERY SHALL PREVAIL...

Next: RETURN OF THE GODDESS

INTO *THE DREAM-TIME* WHERE HIS SPIRIT CREATURE THE PHOENIX... *THE GOLDEN EAGLE OF THE SUN*... FLEW...

...PURSUING *A WHITE HORSE* GALLOPING FAR BELOW HIM.

ACROSS MARSH AND MOUNTAINS... SKY AND STARS HE PURSUED IT...

BUT THE HORSE WAS ALWAYS SWIFTER... ALWAYS AHEAD...

UNTIL HE FLEW FAST AS AN ARROW

AND DIVED INTO THE SUN

BURSTING INTO FLAMES...

AND HEARD ONCE AGAIN THE MUSIC OF THE SINGING STONES AT GLASTONBURY... *THE MUSIC OF THE STARS*

AS HE WAS REBORN FROM HIS OWN ASHES...

THE LIGHT FILLED HIS MIND...
AND HE KNEW THE CEREMONY
WAS NO MEANINGLESS
BARBARISM — BUT A
RECOGNITION THAT THE LIFE
SOURCE WAS **ROYAL** AND
MUST BE **TREASURED.**

A WAY OF **ENSURING** THAT
THE SUN KING — NO MATTER
WHAT HIS TRIBAL WARS —
WOULD **NEVER** HARM THE
EARTH, HIS WIFE...

IF THE DAY EVER CAME
WHEN RULERS FORGOT
THIS, THEN THE EARTH
WAS IN MORTAL
DANGER FROM **TRUE**
BARBARIANS...

THEN HE WAS GLIDING DOWN TO
EARTH... BACK TO HIS OWN NEST...

UKKO!

HEH,
HEH! THE
TREASURE'S
ALL
MINE!

YOU
THIEVING
LITTLE
WEASEL!

SL-SLÁINE!
TH-THERE'S A
PERFECTLY GOOD
EXPLANATION...
ONLY I HAVEN'T
THOUGHT OF
IT YET!

AS SOMEWHERE
IN THE DISTANCE,
HE COULD HEAR
CATHBAD CHANTING...
'SUN KING AND EARTH
GODDESS... MERRY MEET—
MERRY PART...'

NO,
SLÁINE!
NO!

'THE RITE IS ENDED... LET
THE SLEEPER AWAKE!'

SLÁINE...
UUUK! WAKE UP!
IT'S ME—
UKKO!

THE
GODDESS..?

IS GONE. COME...
IT IS TIME FOR YOUR
CORONATION!

Next: THE
FINAL
ACT

WATER HEAT AND WATER BOIL! MAKE THE WHEEL OF HEAVEN TOIL! FIRE FLAME AND FIRE BURN! MAKE THE WHEEL OF HEAVEN TURN!

'...Then he who is to be inaugurated, not as a prince but a beast, comes before the people on all fours, confessing himself a beast also...'

NEIGHHHH!

NOW SLÁINE WAS A STALLION, CONSORT OF THE WHITE HORSE — SYMBOL OF THE EARTH GODDESS...

...MAKING A RITUAL CIRCUIT OF THE ROUND HALL, LIKE THE SUN CIRCLES THE STARS...

...EACH OF HIS WARRIORS' STALLS REPRESENTING A SIGN OF THE ZODIAC.

MEDB LOOKED ON BITTERLY...

HAVE YOUR DAY, SLAINE MAC ROTH... BUT MINE COMES SOON...

FOR THE CAULDRON THAT GAVE YOU YOUR KINGDOM IS ALSO THE CAULDRON OF AVAGDDU — DISEASED SON OF THE GODDESS...

...THE DARK SIDE OF EARTH POWER THAT SHALL DESTROY YOU!

THERE WAS ONLY ROOM FOR THE NOBILITY, BUT I MANAGED TO SQUEEZE IN GERG AND SOME OF THE OTHER CHARIOTEERS...

THREE GOLD PIECES YOU CHARGED US TO SEE THE CORONATION!

AND WE CAN'T SEE A THING!

YES, BUT AT LEAST YOU CAN TELL YOUR GRANDCHILDREN YOU WERE THERE!

UKKO, WHAT DO YOU *DO* WITH THE GOLD YOU COLLECT? YOU CAN'T SPEND IT ALL.

I HOARD IT AND SNUGGLE UP TO IT ON COLD WINTER NIGHTS. IT'S A GREAT COMFORT TO ME.

WEIRD!

'He sits in the cauldron surrounded by his people and he and they eat of the meat which he gives to them...'

EAT THE FLESH OF THE GODDESS — MAY HER STRENGTH BECOME YOUR STRENGTH.

'He is then required to drink of the broth in which he bathes, not in any cup, not even in his hand, but lapping it with his mouth...'

AND THEY THINK *I'M* WEIRD!

'When this unrighteous and outlandish rite is carried out, his Kingship is conferred.'

DO YOU SWEAR AS THE SUN IS ABOVE THE CLOUDS OF THE EARTH, SO YOUR SOUL SHALL BE ABOVE THE CLOUDS OF FEAR?

I SWEAR THEY WILL ROLL DARK BENEATH ME.

CATHBAD PUT THE ROYAL CLOAK OF GOLDEN EAGLE FEATHERS AROUND HIM...

I HEREBY PROCLAIM YOU SUN KING! LET US REJOICE IN THE ROBE OF YOUR BEAMS!

THEN THE DRUID LAID GEIS UPON HIM... MAGIC TABOOS, BASED ON PAST EVENTS THAT BROUGHT MISFORTUNE TO THE TRIBE...

YOU ARE FORBIDDEN TO... LISTEN TO THE BIRDS OF LOUGH SWILLY WHEN THE SUN SETS. DRINK THE WATERS OF BO NEMRIDH BETWEEN DAWN AND DARKNESS. EAT DOG. WEAR A CLOAK OF MANY COLOURS ON A DAPPLED HORSE ON THE HEATH OF LONRAD. STILL BE IN BED AT SUNRISE ON LUGNASAD.

...IF A KING BROKE HIS GEIS IT WOULD LEAD TO DISASTER AND DEATH.

AS THE REJOICING BEGAN...

AND IT IS MY FIRST DECREE THAT MY DWARF UKKO SHOULD BE APPOINTED TO A POST HE IS MOST SUITED AND QUALIFIED FOR...

THE POST OF ROYAL PARASITE.

OH, SIRE! I AM TRULY HONOURED!

THE PARASITE'S TASK WAS TO AMUSE AND PRAISE THE KING...

YOU WILL ENTERTAIN ME UNTIL THE TIME FOR MY DEATH, WHEN YOU SHALL BE KILLED ALSO... SO YOU CAN MAKE ME HAPPY AFTER DEATH.

EH?

I-I BEG TO DECLINE, SIRE! THAT—THAT WOULD BE TOO GREAT AN HONOUR!

BUT I INSIST, UKKO. I KNOW YOU COULDN'T BEAR TO BE PARTED FROM ME. IT WILL BE YOUR REWARD FOR BEING MY COMPANION ALL THESE YEARS.

I SHALL LEAVE SPECIAL INSTRUCTIONS FOR YOU TO BE THE FIRST TO BE THROWN ON MY FUNERAL PYRE—EVEN BEFORE MY HUMAN WIFE AND CONCUBINES.

THEN I BEGAN MY DUTIES AS ROYAL PARASITE AND SANG THE KING'S PRAISES...

LET US SALUTE HIM! THE BATTLE-EAGER AXEMAN WHOSE HEROIC HARD HAND SPLASHES GORE! FOR IT WAS *SLÁINE* WHO DEFEATED THE GULEDIG OF CYTHRAUL! *SLÁINE* WHO ESCAPED FROM THE TOWER OF GLASS! *SLÁINE* WHO KILLED THE ICE DRAGON OF THE GLAMOURLAND! HE WAS A RAGING STORM! A CRIMSON BLADE! NOT SOMEONE TO BEHOLD ON A DARK NIGHT!

AND I SWEAR BY THE GODS WE SWEAR BY! I WILL PROVIDE *MORE* CHOPPED FLESH FOR THE MAGGOT GOD! I WILL DRIVE THE TYRANTS BACK TO TORY ISLAND! *SO THE LAND OF THE YOUNG IS FREE AGAIN!*

SLÁINE the King

SCRIPT:
PAT MILLS
ART:
GLENN FABRY
LETTERING:
STEVE POTTER

AND I, TOO, WAS THERE—
CHEERING THEM ON...

BE CAREFUL,
SLÁINE.
REMEMBER YOU'VE A
TRIBE AND DWARF
TO SUPPORT.

...IN THIS WAY, SLÁINE'S *RED*—OR VIOLENT—*BRANCH*
WERE INCITED TO NEW HEIGHTS OF SAVAGERY.

REMEMBER
OUR WEDDING
VOWS, SLÁINE...
PROTECT ME...
LOVE ME...

AND THERE WAS FURTHER
ENCOURAGEMENT (IF ANY
WAS NEEDED) FROM *THE
EARTH GODDESS*
WATCHING FROM THE
EL WORLDS...

...AS SLÁINE'S HEAVENLY WIFE
BLODEUWEDD— 'FLOWER FACE'...

THE EARTH MAIDEN HE LOVED EVEN MORE THAN NIAMH...

AND THE THOUGHT OF HER BEAUTY BEING DEFILED
BY THE LOATHSOME DWELLERS FROM THE DEEP...
THE FOUL THINGS FROM TORY ISLAND...

BROUGHT ON HIS
WARP SPASM.

AND HER POWER POURED INTO HIM SO HE
SWELLED INTO A MONSTROUS CREATURE...
SO MASSIVE, A WARRIOR'S FOOT WOULD
FIT BETWEEN EACH RIB...

NO MYTH... NO
WILD EXAGGERATION...
NO ALE TALKING...

IN THOSE DAYS MEN
REALLY COULD WARP
THE SERPENT POWER
THROUGH THEIR BODIES.

Sláine
the King

GWALCHAZED THE RAM CHALLENGED DUNDAN SKULLSMASHER FOR THE HERO'S PORTION.

In former times, when the hindquarters were served the bravest hero took the thigh-piece and if another Celt claimed it, they stood up and fought in a single combat to the death.

SCRIPT: PAT MILLS
ART: GLENN FABRY
LETTERING: STEVE POTTER

I CLAIM THE HERO'S PORTION.

GOOD. WELL, NOW THAT'S DECIDED. PERHAPS WE CAN GET ON WITH OUR DINNER BEFORE IT GETS COLD.

AFTER THE MEAL, SLÁINE REMAINED IN A DARK MOOD— DESPITE MY EFFORTS AS *ROYAL PARASITE* TO BRING A SMILE TO HIS FACE...

HOW ABOUT SOME *RIDDLES?* I LOOK AT YOU WHENEVER YOU LOOK AT ME. YOU SEE, BUT I SEE NOT. I SPEAK, BUT HAVE NO VOICE. MY LIPS CAN ONLY OPEN USELESSLY.

SO WHAT AM I?

A MIRROR!

ANOTHER, UKKO!

ALL RIGHT... SEE NOT AND YOU WILL SEE ME. SO WHAT AM I?

DARKNESS!

ONE MORE! ...SPEAK NOT AND THOU SHALT SPEAK MY NAME!

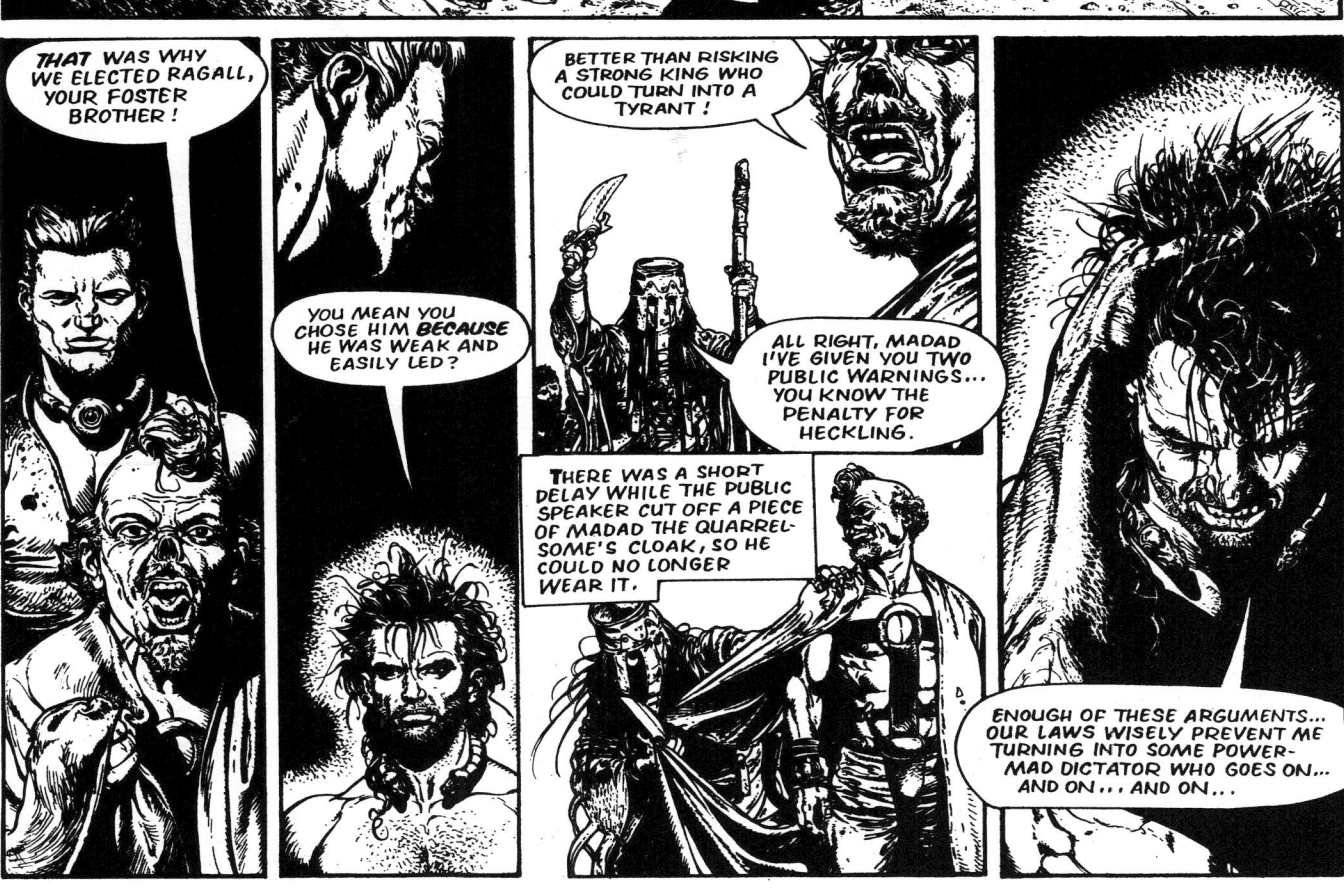

SLÁINE RETURNS IN
THE HORNED GOD